W9-DEK-991

The Story of My Typewriter

The Story of My Typewriter

Paul Auster

Sam Messer

D.A.P.
New York

D.A.P. / Distributed Art Publishers, Inc.

Published in the United States by
D.A.P. / Distributed Art Publishers, Inc.
155 Sixth Ave., 2nd Floor
New York NY 10013

Printed in China

Library of Congress Control Number 00 - 132989

ISBN 1-891024-32-9

First Edition

ISBN 1-891024-43-4 (Limited Edition)

Artwork photographed by Susan Einstein, Los Angeles
Production Manager: Lori Waxman

Book Design by Craig Willis

Olympia
clear
set

THE ART OF HUNGER
DISAPPEARANCES
SELECTED POEMS
GHOSTS
TIMBUKTU
NEW YORK TRILOGY
AUSTER
SMOKE
CHANCE
CITY OF GLASS
LOCKED ROOM
HAND TO MO
MR. VERTIGO
Paul Auster
MOON PALACE
THE INVENTION OF SOLITUDE
LEVIATHAN
WHY WRITE
De Luxe
Olympia

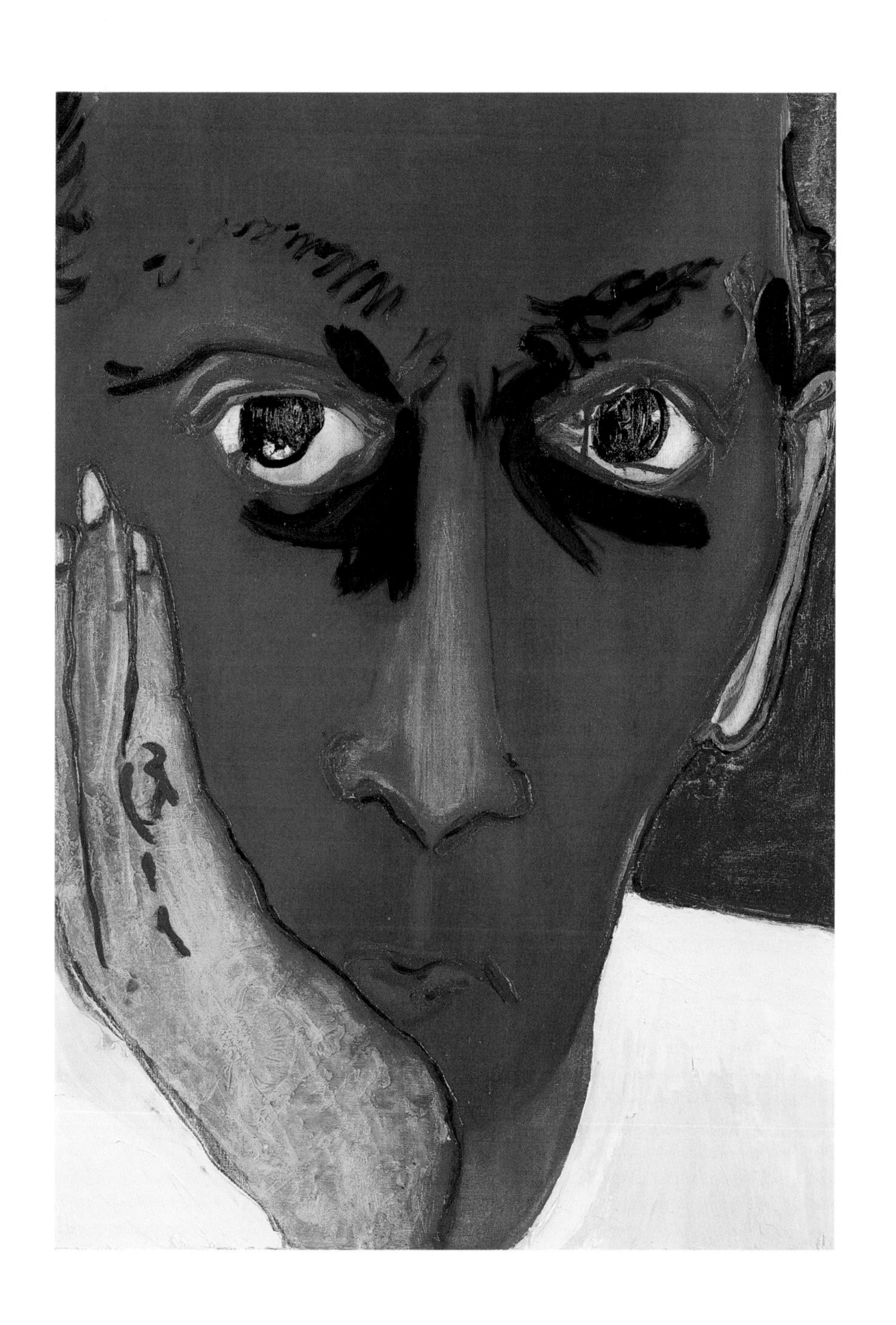

Three and a half years later, I came home to America. It was July 1974, and when I unpacked my bags that first afternoon in New York, I discovered that my little Hermes typewriter had been destroyed. The cover was smashed in, the keys were mangled and twisted out of shape, and there was no hope of ever having it repaired.

I couldn't afford to buy a new typewriter. I rarely had much money in those days, but at that particular moment I was dead broke.

A couple of nights later, an old college friend invited me to his apartment for dinner. At some point during our conversation, I mentioned what had happened to my typewriter, and he told me that he had one in the closet that he didn't use anymore. It had been given to him as a graduation present from junior high school in 1962. If I wanted to buy it from him, he said, he would be glad to sell it to me.

We agreed on a price of forty dollars. It was an Olympia portable, manufactured in West Germany. That country no longer exists, but since that day in 1974, every word I have written has been typed out on that machine.

=234567890-¾
+"#$%_&'()*!
QWERTYUIP^
qwertyuiop`
ASDFGHJKL:ç
asdfghjkl;é
ZXCVBNM,.?
zxcvbnm,./

I remember pointing out the typewriter to him the first time he visited, but I can't remember what he said. A day or two after that, he came back to the house. I wasn't around that afternoon, but he asked my wife if he could go downstairs to my work room and have a look at my typewriter. God knows what he did down there, but there is no doubt in my mind that the typewriter spoke to him. In due course, I believe he managed to persuade it to bare its soul to him.
He has been back several times since,

CITY OF GLASS
TIMBUKTU
MR. VERTIGO

In the beginning, I didn't think about it much. A year went by, ten years went by, and not once did I consider it odd or even vaguely unusual to be working with a manual typewriter. The only alternative was an electric typewriter, but I didn't like the noise those contraptions made: the constant hum of the motor, the buzzing and rattling of loose parts, the jitterbug pulse of alternating current vibrating in my fingers. I preferred the stillness of my Olympia. It was comfortable to the touch, it worked smoothly, it was dependable. And when I wasn't pounding on the keyboard, it was silent.

Best of all, it seemed to be indestructible. Except for changing ribbons and occasionally having to brush out the ink buildup from the keys, I was absolved of all maintenance duties. Since 1974, I have changed the roller twice, perhaps three times. I have taken it into the shop for cleaning no more than I have voted in Presidential elections. I have never had to replace any parts. The only serious trauma it has suffered occurred in 1979 when my two-year-old son snapped off the carriage return arm. But that wasn't the typewriter's fault. I was in despair for the rest of the day, but the next morning I carried it to a shop on Court Street and had the arm soldered back in place. There is a small scar on that spot now, but the operation was a success, and the arm has held ever since.

TAB
clear
set.

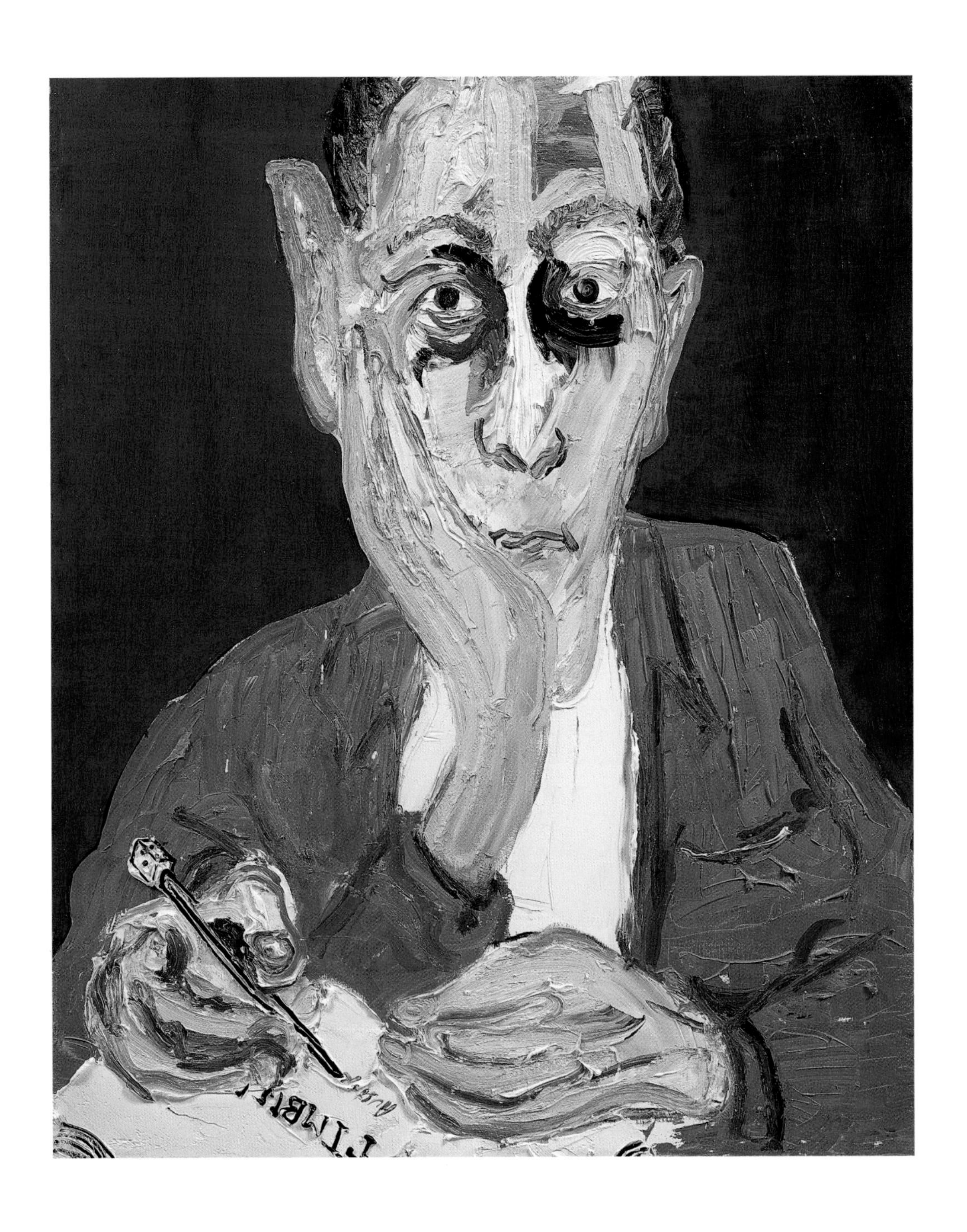

There is no point in talking about computers and word processors. Early on, I was tempted to buy one of those marvels for myself, but too many friends told me horror stories about pushing the wrong button and wiping out a day's work—or a month's work—and I heard one too many warnings about sudden power failures that could erase an entire manuscript in less than half a second. I have never been good with machines, and I knew that if there was a wrong button to be pushed, I would eventually push it.

So I held on to my old typewriter, and the 1980s became the 1990s. One by one, all my friends switched over to Macs and IBMs. I began to look like an enemy of progress, the last pagan holdout in a world of digital converts. My friends made fun of me for resisiting the new ways. When they weren't calling me a curmudgeon, they called me a reactionary and a stubborn old goat. I didn't care. What was good for them wasn't necessarily good for me, I said. Why should I change when I was perfectly happy as I was?

Until then, I hadn't felt particularily attached to my typewriter. It was simply a tool that allowed me to do my work, but now that it had become an endangered species, one of the last surviving artifacts of twentieth-century *homo scriptorus*, I began to develop a certain affection for it. Like it or not, I realized, we had the same past. As time went on, I came to understand that we also had the same future.

Two or three years ago, sensing that the end was near, I went to Leon, my local stationer in Brooklyn, and asked him to order fifty typewriter ribbons for me. He had to call around for several days to scare up an order of that size. Some of them, he later told me, were shipped in from as far away as Kansas City.

I use these ribbons as cautiously as I can, typing on them until the ink is all but invisible on the page. When the supply is gone, I have little hope that there will be any ribbons left.

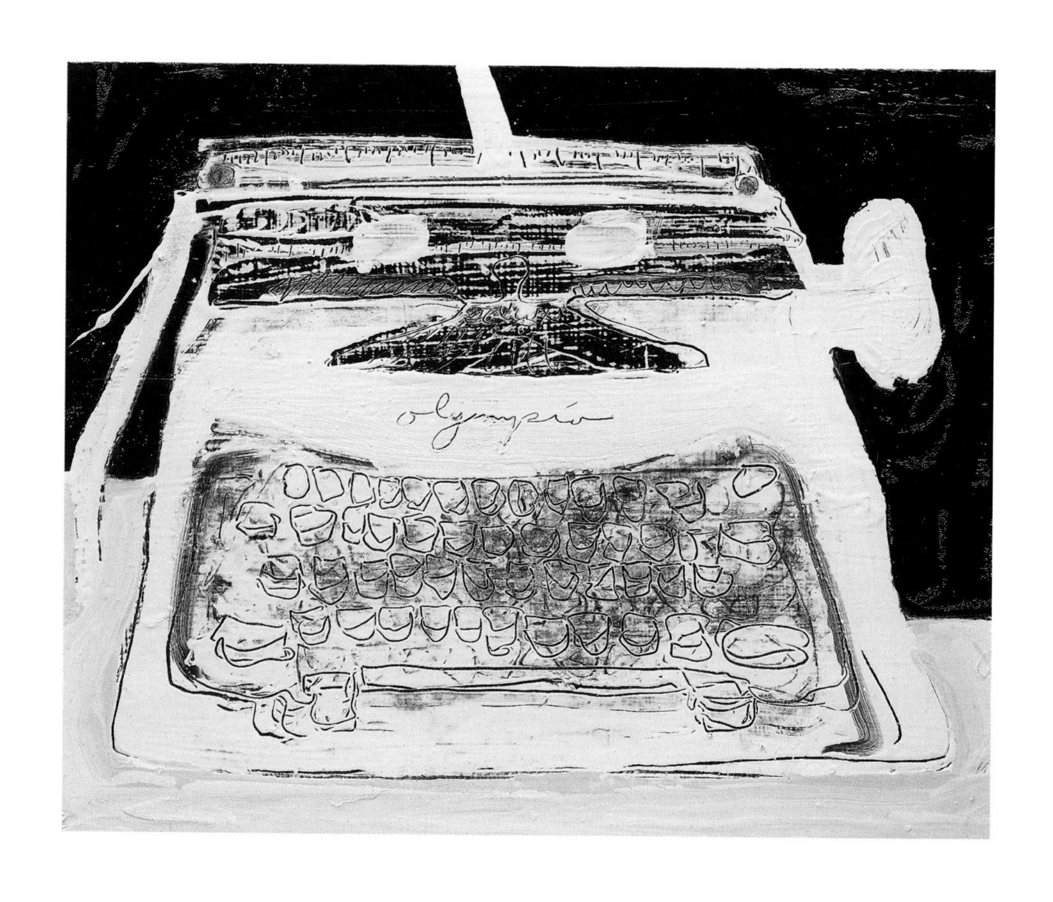
olympia

olympia

MY NAME IS PAUL AUSTER (That is not MY REAL NAME!)
SWIFT AND LEARN

It was never my intention to turn my typewriter into a heroic figure. That is the work of Sam Messer, a man who stepped into my house one day and fell in love with a machine. There is no accounting for the passions of artists. The affair has lasted for several years now, and right from the beginning, I suspect that the feelings have been mutual.

Messer seldom goes anywhere without a sketchbook. He draws constantly, stabbing at the page with furious, rapid strokes, looking up from his pad every other second to squint at the person or object before him, and whenever you sit down to a meal with him, you do so with the understanding that you are also posing for your portrait. We have been through this routine so many times in the past seven or eight years that I no longer think about it.

I remember pointing out the typewriter to him the first time he visited, but I can't remember what he said. A day or two after that, he came back to the house. I wasn't around that afternoon, but he asked my wife if he could go downstairs to my work room and have another look at the typewriter. God knows what he did down there, but I have never doubted that the typewriter spoke to him. In due course, I believe he even managed to persuade it to bare its soul.

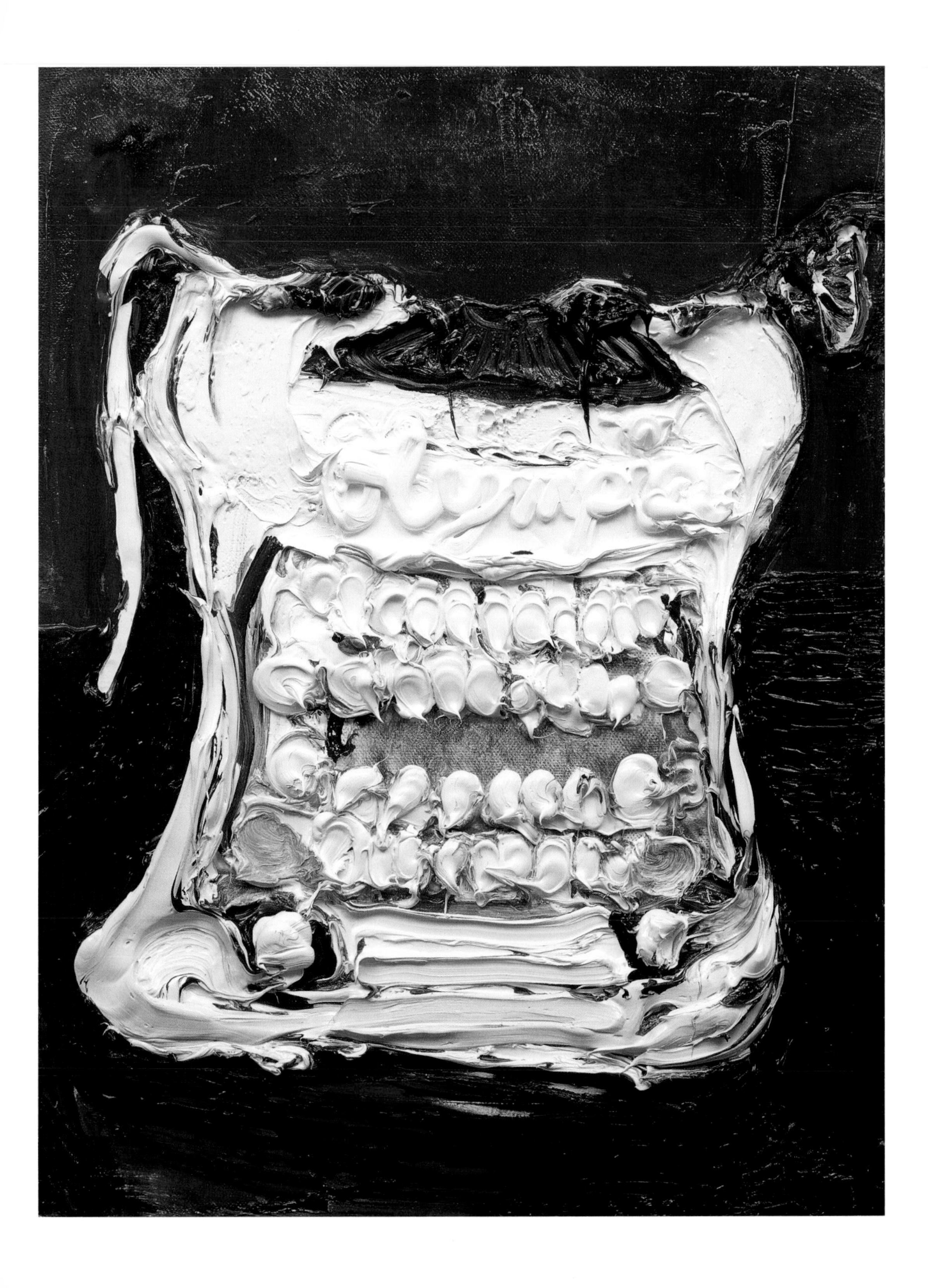

He has been back several times since, and each visit has produced a fresh wave of paintings, drawings, and photographs. Sam has taken possession of my typewriter, and little by little he has turned an inanimate object into a being with a personality and a presence in the world. The typewriter has moods and desires now, it expresses dark angers and exuberant joys, and trapped within its gray, metallic body, you would almost swear that you could hear the beating of a heart.

I have to admit that I find all this unsettling. The paintings are brilliantly done, and I am proud of my typewriter for proving itself to be such a worthy subject, but at the same time Messer has forced me to look at my old companion in a new way. I am still in the process of adjustment, but whenever I look at one of these paintings now (there are two of them hanging on my living room wall), I have trouble thinking of my typewriter as an *it*. Slowly but surely, the *it* has turned into a *him*.

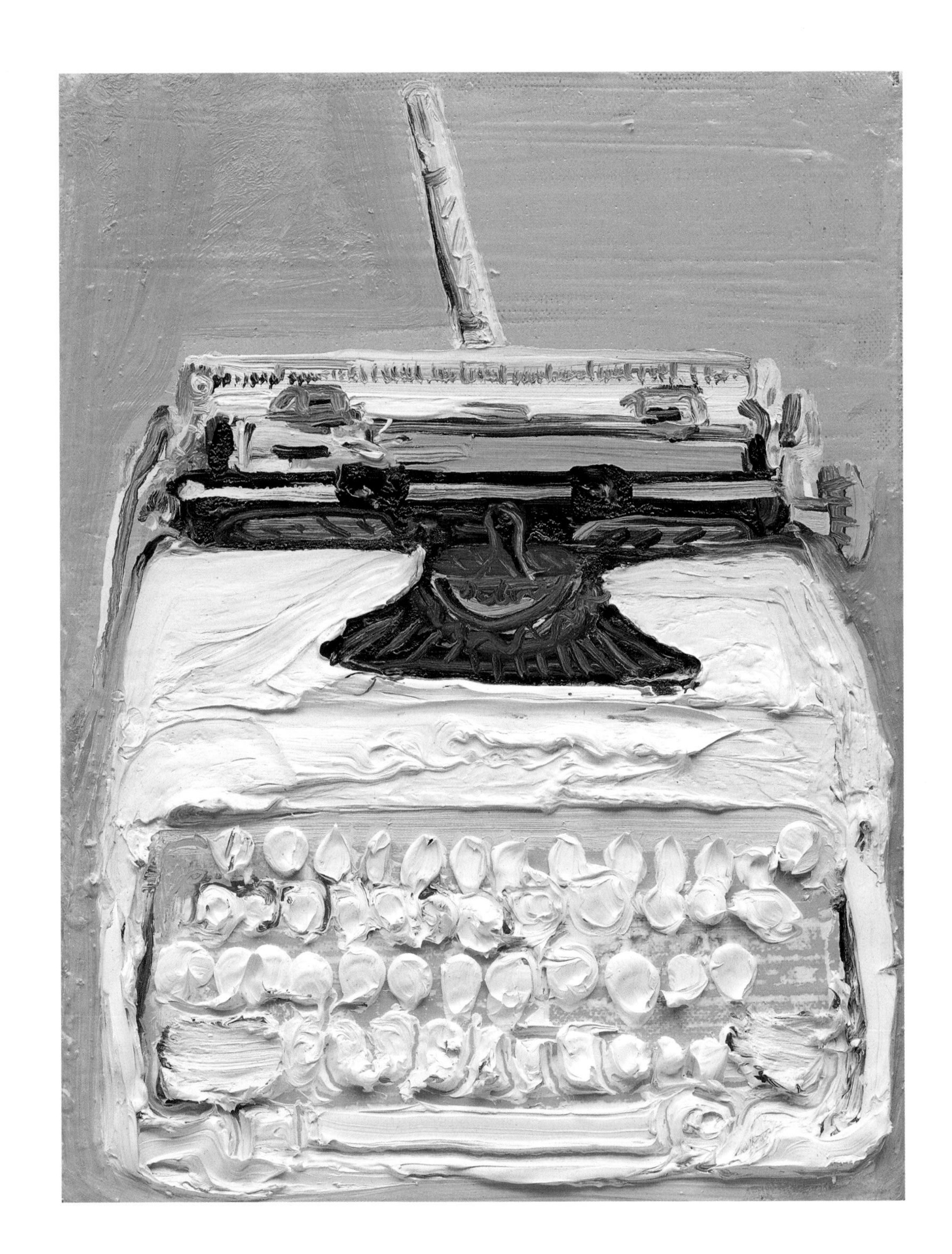

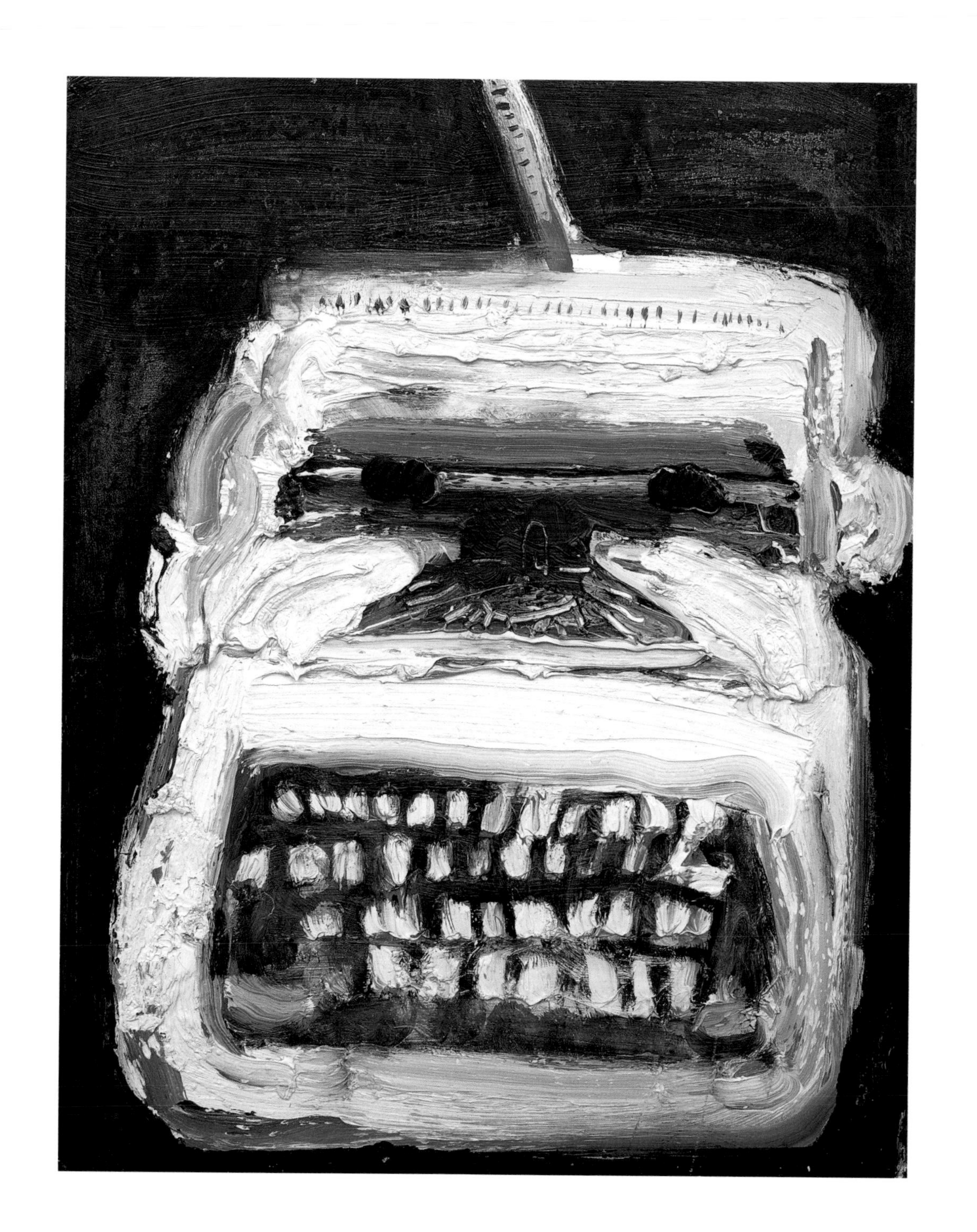

olympia

Olympia
TAB
MR
clear
set

We have been together for more than a quarter of a century now. Everywhere I have gone, the typewriter has gone with me. We have lived in Manhattan, in upstate New York, and in Brooklyn. We have traveled together to California and to Maine, to Minnesota and to Massachusetts, to Vermont and to France. In that time, I have written with hundreds of pencils and pens. I have owned several cars, several refrigerators, and have occupied several apartments and houses. I have worn out dozens of pairs of shoes, have given up on scores of sweaters and jackets, have lost or abandoned watches, alarm clocks, and umbrellas. Everything breaks, everything wears out, everything loses its purpose in the end, but the typewriter is still with me. It is the only object I own today that I owned twenty-six years ago. In another few months, it will have been with me for exactly half my life.

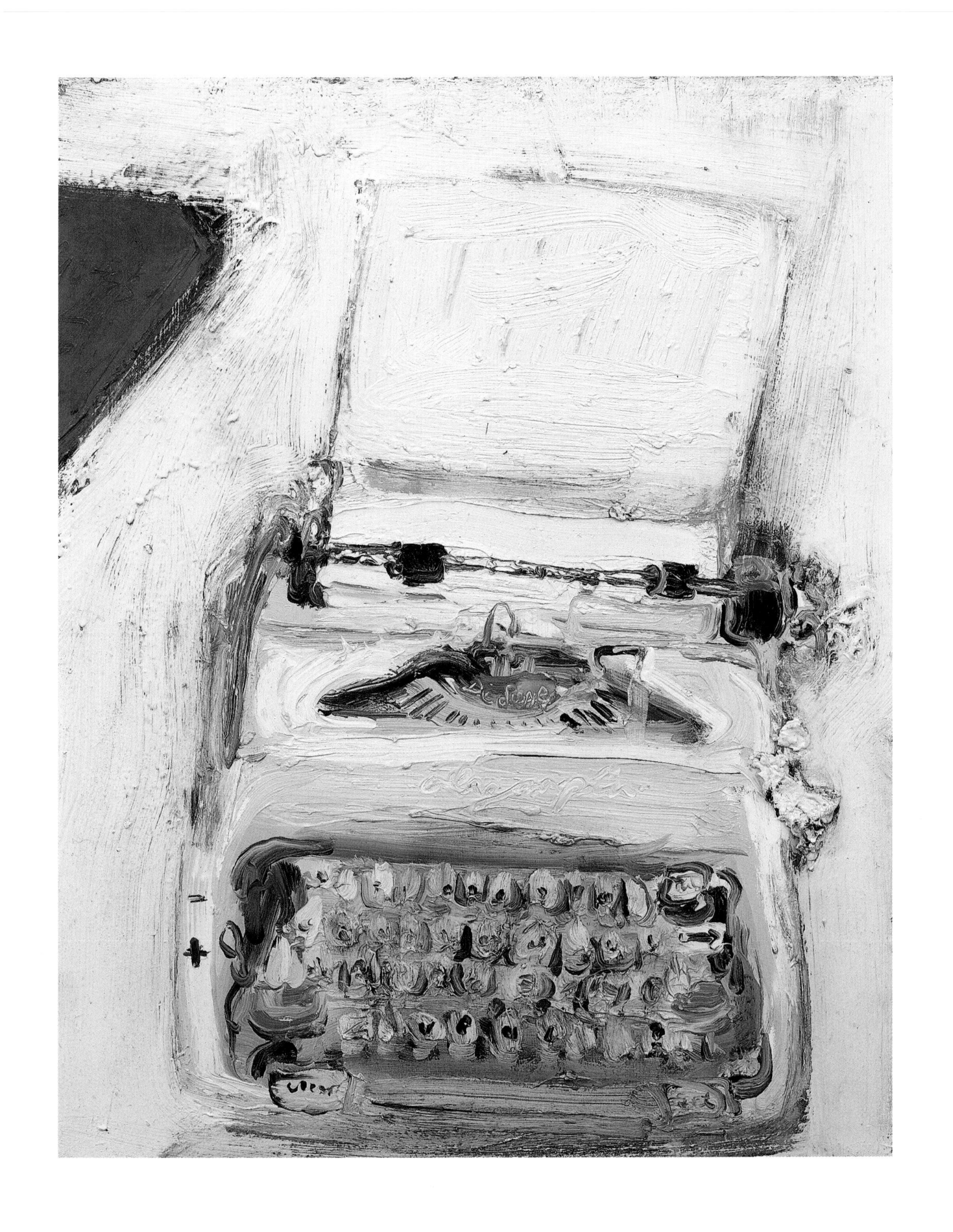

2 3 4 5
Q W E R T
A S D F
Z X C V

7 8 9 0
Y U I O P
H J K L
B N M

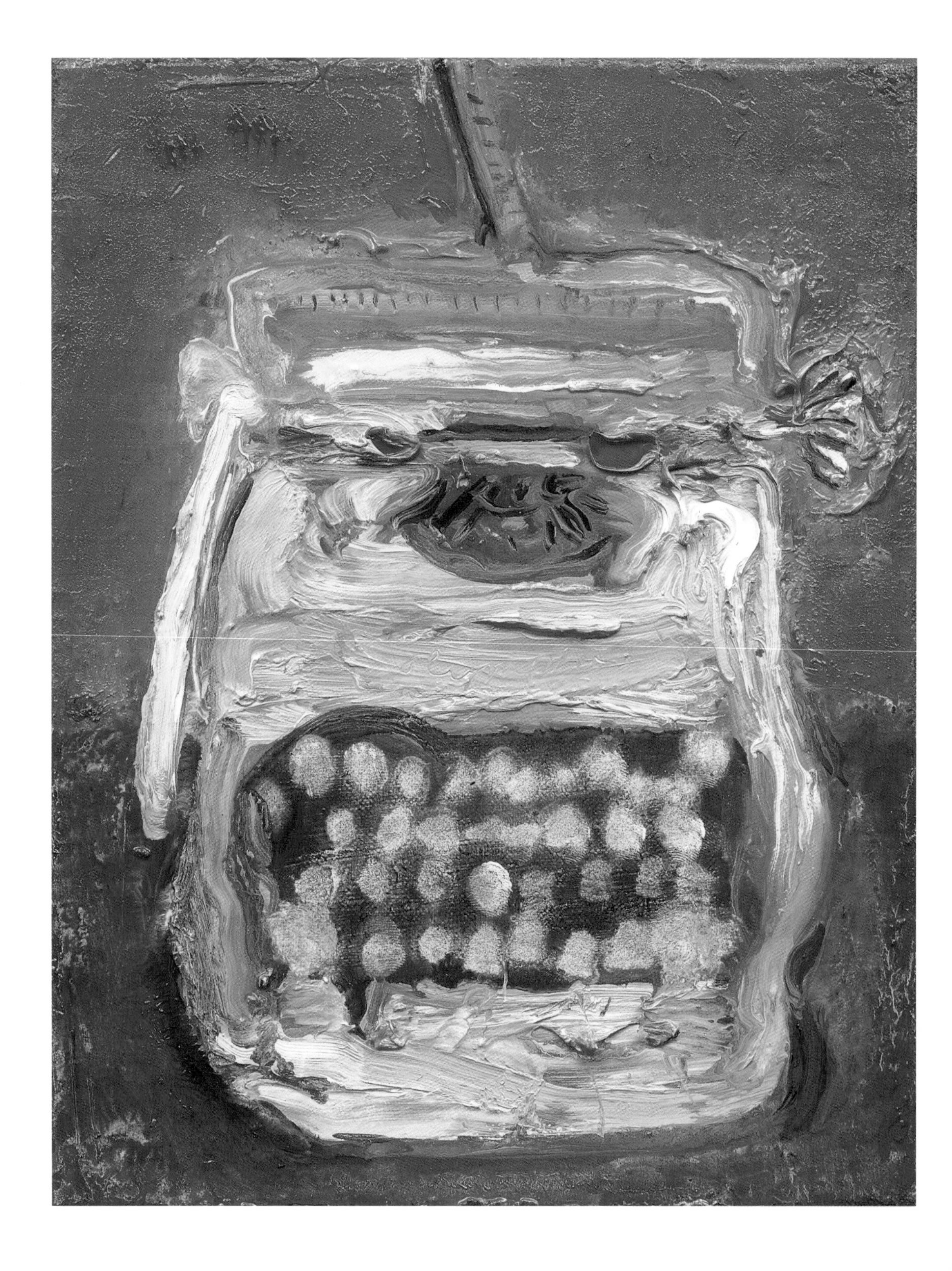

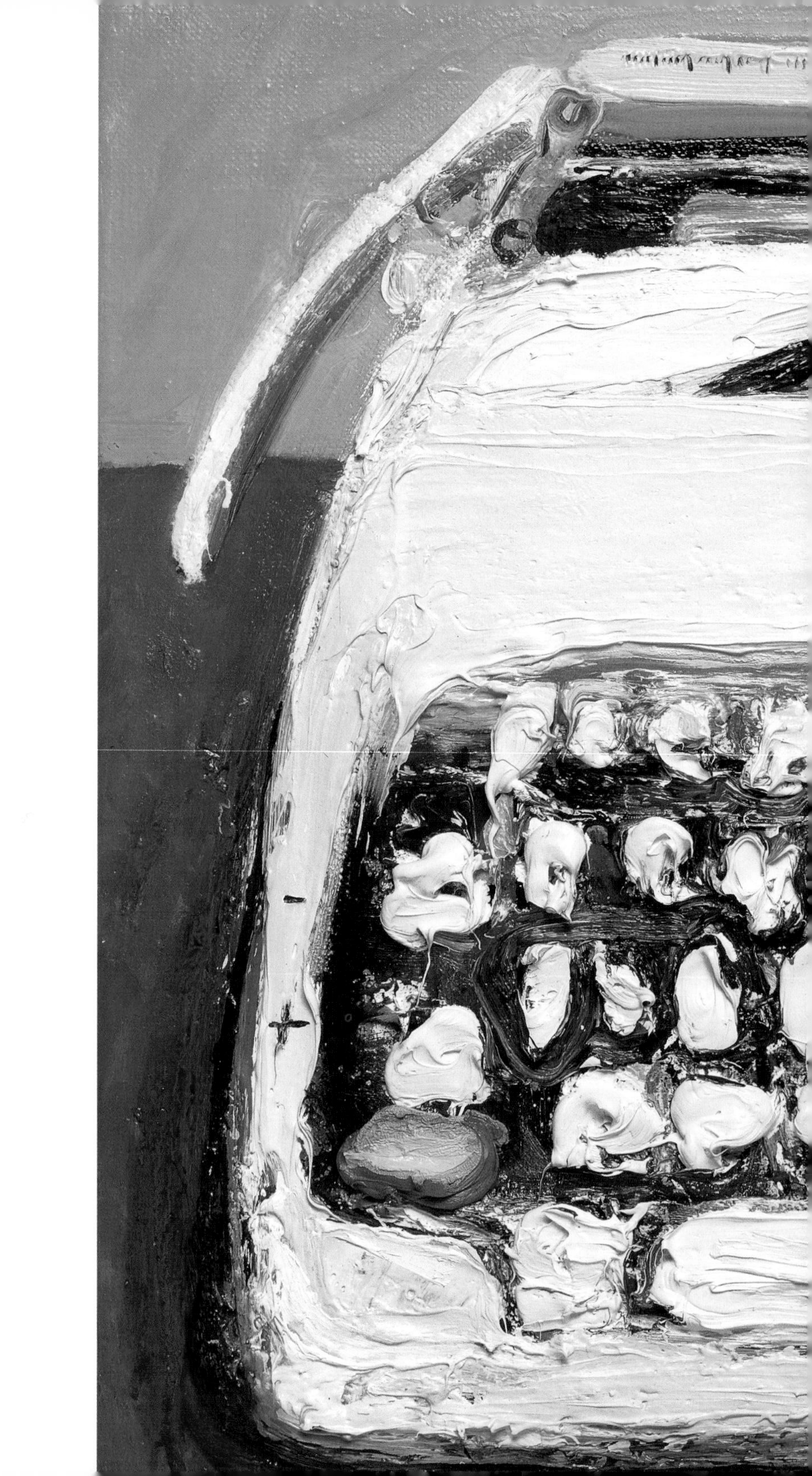

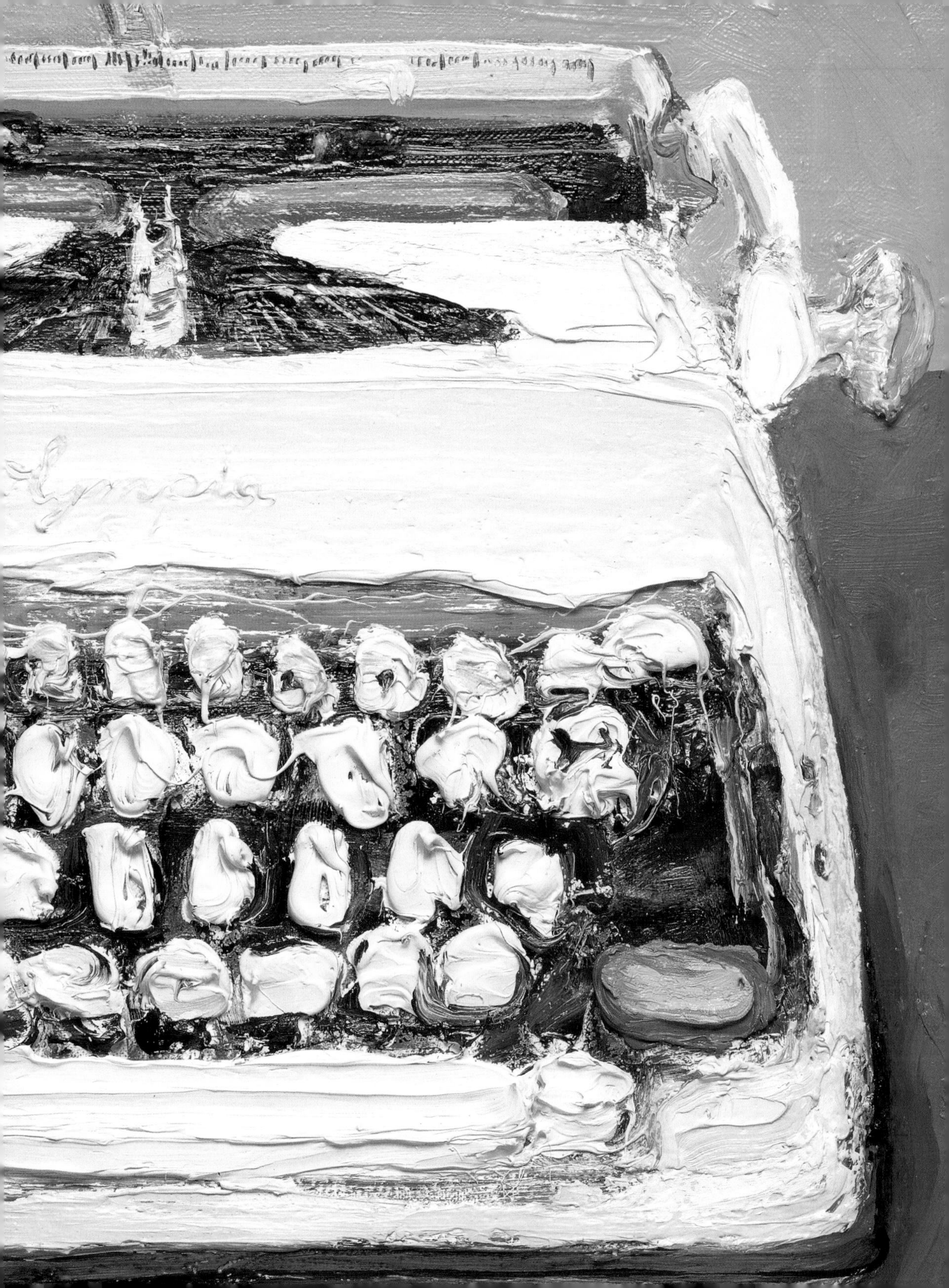

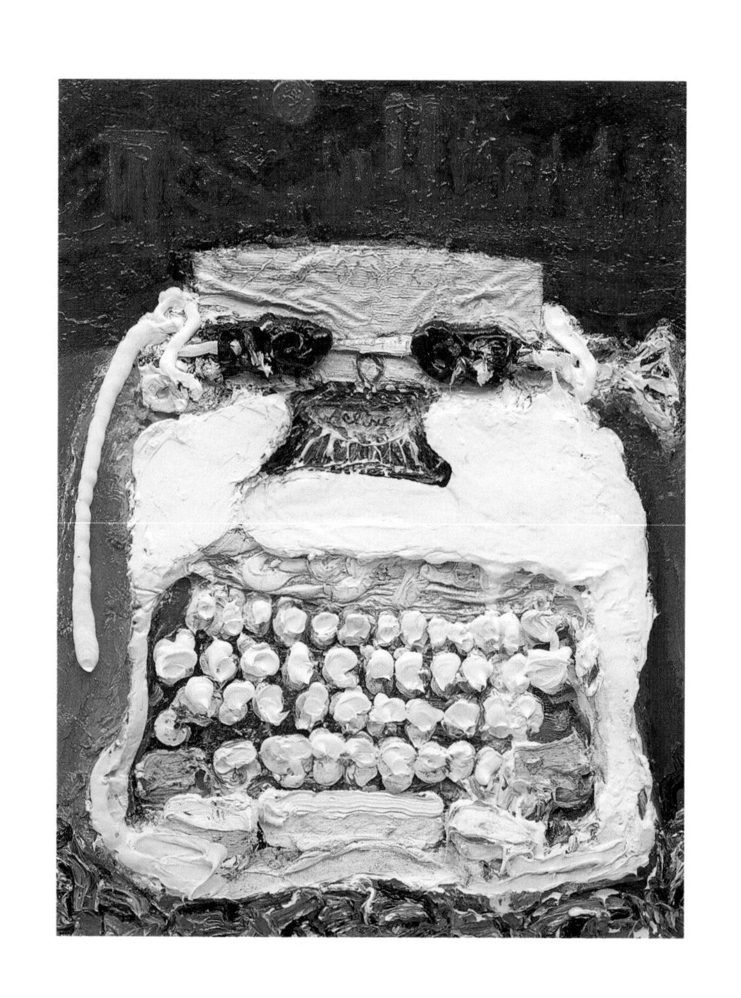

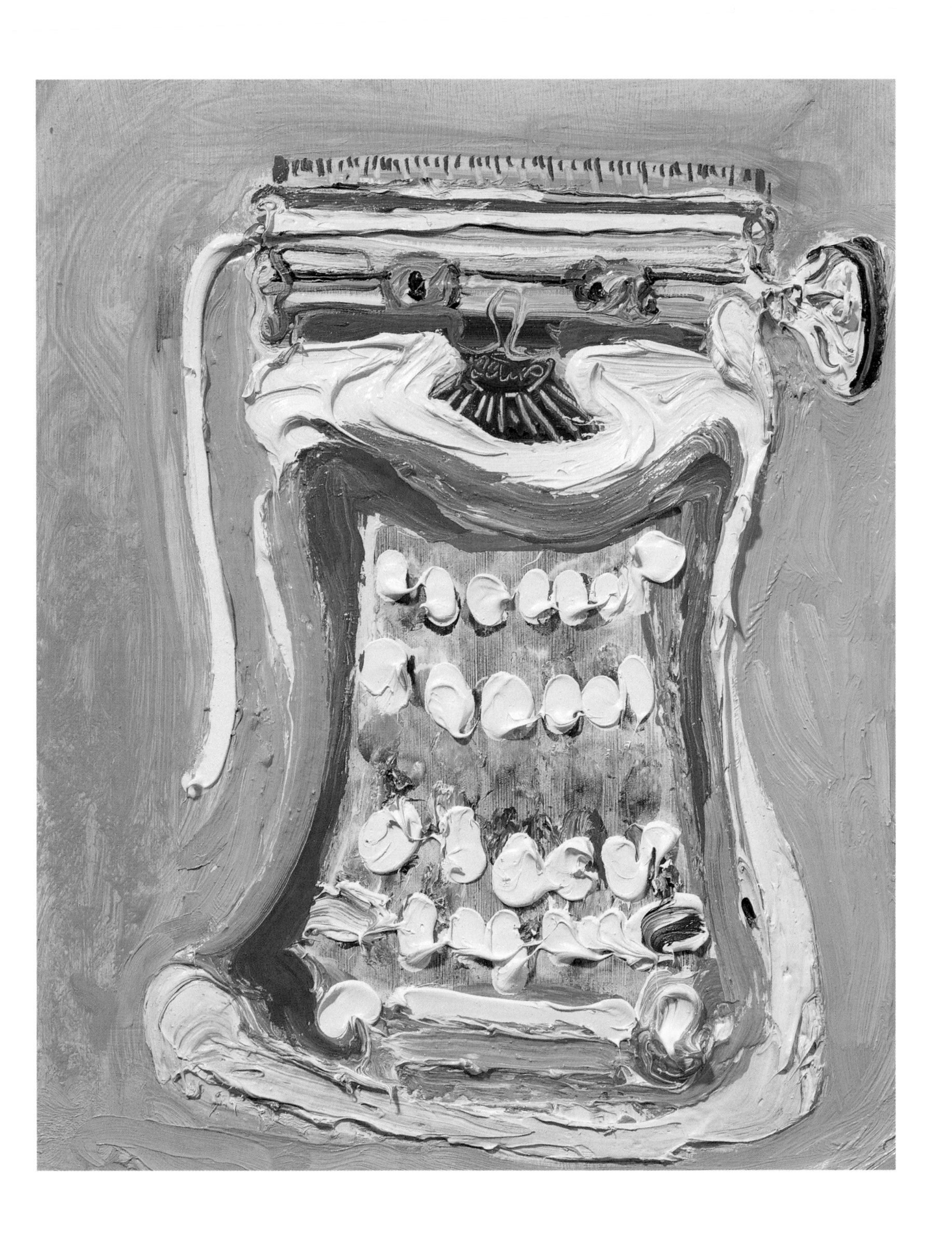

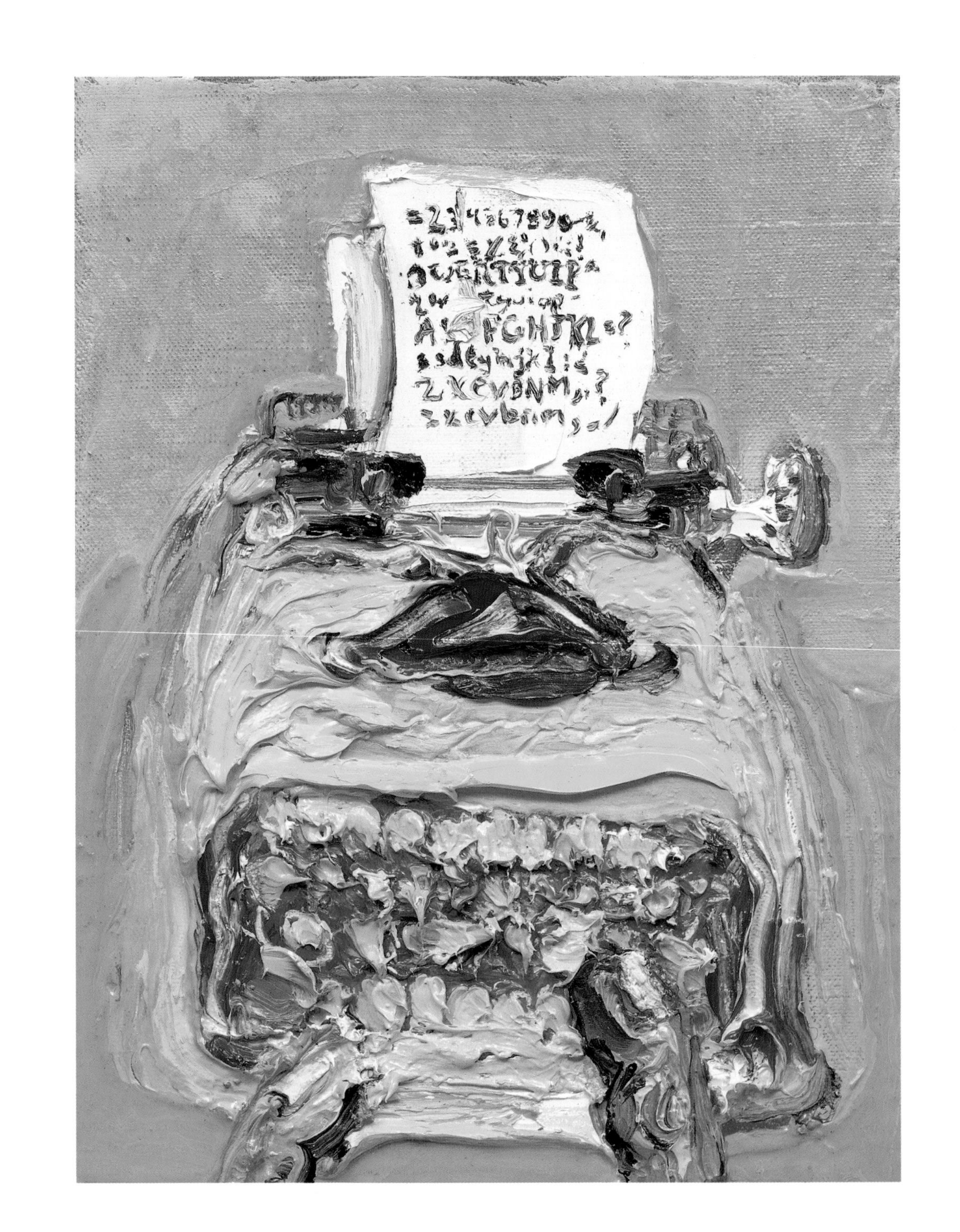

Battered and obsolete, a relic from an age that is quickly passing from memory, the damn thing has never given out on me. Even as I recall the nine thousand four hundred days we have spent together, it is sitting in front of me now, stuttering forth its old familiar music. We are in Connecticut for the weekend. It is summer, and the morning outside the window is hot and green and beautiful. The typewriter is on the kitchen table, and my hands are on the typewriter. Letter by letter, I have watched it write these words.

July 2, 2000

PAUL AUSTER

Novels

The New York Trilogy (City of Glass, 1985 • Ghosts, 1986 • The Locked Room, 1986) • In the Country of Last Things, 1987 • Moon Palace, 1989 • The Music of Chance, 1990 • Leviathan, 1992 • Mr. Vertigo, 1994 • Timbuktu, 1999

Non-Fiction

White Spaces, 1980 • The Invention of Solitude, 1982 • The Art of Hunger, 1982/1992 • Why Write?, 1996 • Hand to Mouth, 1997

Screenplays

Smoke & Blue in the Face: Two Films, 1995 • Lulu on the Bridge, 1998

Poetry

Unearth, 1974 • Wall Writing, 1976 • Fragments from Cold, 1977 • Facing the Music, 1980 • Disappearances: Selected Poems, 1988

Editor

The Random House Book of Twentieth-Century French Poetry, 1982 • I Thought My Father Was God and Other True Tales from NPR's National Story Project, 2001

Translations

Fits and Starts: Selected Poems of Jacques Dupin, 1974 • The Uninhabited: Selected Poems of André du Bouchet, 1976 • The Notebooks of Joseph Joubert, 1983 • A Tomb for Anatole, by Stéphane Mallarmé, 1983 • On the High Wire, by Philippe Petit, 1985 • Vicious Circles, by Maurice Blanchot, 1985 • Joan Miró: Selected Writings, 1986 • Translations, 1996 • Chronicle of Guayaki Indians, by Pierre Clastres, 1997

SAM MESSER

Selected Public Collections

The Art Institute of Chicago • Archer J. Huntington Art Gallery, University of Texas • David Winton Bell Gallery, List Art Center, Brown University, Providence, RI • DeCordova Museum and Sculpture Park, Lincoln, MA • Fort Lauderdale Museum of Art, Fort Lauderdale, FL • The Metropolitan Museum of Art, New York • The Museum of Fine Arts, Boston • The Museum of Fine Arts, Houston • Museo Rufino Tamayo, Mexico City • Neuberger Museum, Purchase, NY • Rose Museum, Brandeis College, Waltham, MA • Wadsworth Atheneum, Hartford, CT • Wellington Management, Boston, MA • Yale University Art Gallery Museum, New Haven, CT • The Whitney Museum of American Art, New York

Honors and Awards

Guggenheim Fellowship • Pollock-Krasner Foundation Award • Academy of Arts and Letters Purchase Award • Moonhole Artist Colony Award • The Engelhard Award • Louis Comfort Tiffany Foundation Grant • National Studio Program, Institute for Art and Urban Resources, P.S.1 Fellowship • The Fine Arts Work Center in Provincetown Fellowship • Skowhegan School of Painting and Sculpture

Academic Affiliations

Senior Art Critic, Yale University School of Art Painting Department • Director Yale/Norfolk Summer School of Music and Art, Art Division

PLATES

(All dimensions are in inches. Works are courtesy of the artist unless otherwise noted.)

36 Pink Olympia, oil on canvas, 64 x 78, 2001. The Edward R. Broida collection. Courtesy of the Nielson Gallery.

37 Deluxe, oil on canvas, 68 x 88, 2002. Courtesy of Nielsen Gallery, Boston, MA

38 Maestro, oil on canvas, 58 x 48, 2002

41 First Typewriter, oil on canvas, 16 x 12, 1998. Collection of Paul Auster and Siri Hustvedt, Brooklyn, NY

42 The Wizard of Brooklyn, oil on canvas, 78 x 109, 2001

43 Olympia, oil on canvas, 76 x 105, 2001

44 Olympia (detail)

46 RAVE, oil on canvas, 11 x 8.5, 2001. Collection of Susan Einstein, Los Angeles, CA

47 Tokyo, oil on linen, 11 x 8.5, 2001

48 Los Angeles, oil on linen, 14 x 18, 2001

50 Gotham Olympia, oil on panel, 16 x 12, 2001. Private Collection, Boston, MA. Courtesy of Nielsen Gallery, Boston, MA

51 Gotham Olympia (detail)

53 Forest Hills, Queens, oil on panel, 16 x 12, 2002

54 Arizona, oil on canvas, 11 x 8.5, 2001. Private Collection, Boston, MA. Courtesy of Nielsen Gallery, Boston, MA

57 As One, oil on canvas, 58 x 48, 2002

59 Silent, oil on panel, 22 x 14, 2000

60 Broke, pencil on paper, 20.5 x 16, 1998

62 Self Portrait in collaboration with Josephine Messer, pencil on paper, 11 x 8.5, 2002

64 Partners, charcoal on gessoed canvas, 58 x 96, 2001

68 Typewriter, cast bronze, 1.5 x 2.5 x 3.5, 2000.

70 New York/New York, oil on panel, 22 x 14, 2000

I want to thank Phyllis O'Mara, Nina Nielsen, John Baker, Sid Singer, Mickey Cartin, Ira Riklis, Richard Benson, Nielsen Gallery, Shoshana Wayne Gallery, and Simon Bax for being so supportive over the years. I also want to thank Kiki Smith for being a constant inspiration and for giving me a home on the East Coast.

This book is for Eleanor and Josephine, who make everything extraordinary.

Sam Messer
September 10, 2001
Santa Monica, CA

The Story of My Typewriter

The title pages of this book were set by Paul Auster's Olympia typewriter. The text of this book is composed in Bodoni and Berthold Bodoni Antiqua. Originally designed by Giambattista Bodoni (1740-1813), the Bodoni types were the first of the Modern type designs and express the beginning of the Industrial Revolution; its serifs are flat, thin, and unbracketed, while the stress is always on the mathematically vertical strokes. Berthold Bodoni Antiqua was produced in 1930 and is based on the late eighteenth-century Modern Serif Bodoni. This book is printed on acid free Japanese Matte paper. It was printed and bound in China and manufactured by Asia Pacific Offset in a trade edition of 5000 copies. A limited edition is signed by the author and the artist and includes a miniature bronze interpretation of Paul Auster's typewriter by Sam Messer.